Text © 2022 Sarah Nelson

Illustrations © 2022 Ellen Rooney

Owlkids Books acknowledges the financial support of the Canada Council for the Arts, the Ontario Arts Council,
the Government of Canada through the Canada Book Fund (CBF) and the Government
of Ontario through the Ontario Creates Book Initiative for our publishing activities.

Published in Canada by Owlkids Books Inc., 1 Eglinton Avenue East, Toronto, ON M4P 3A1

Published in the US by Owlkids Books Inc., 1700 Fourth Street, Berkeley, CA 94710

Library of Congress Control Number: 2021941759

LIBRARY AND ARCHIVES CANADA CATALOGUING IN PUBLICATION

Title: A park connects us / Sarah Nelson ; illustrations by Ellen Rooney.

Names: Nelson, Sarah, 1973- author. | Rooney, Ellen, illustrator.

Identifiers: Canadiana 20210250542 | ISBN 9781771474504 (hardcover)

Classification: LCC PZ7.1.N45 Par 2022 | DDC j813/.6—dc23

Edited by Stacey Roderick | Designed by Elisa Gutiérrez

Manufactured in Shenzhen, Guangdong, China, in September 2021, by WKT Co.

Job #21CB1197

A     B     C     D     E     F

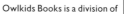

Sarah Nelson

# A Park Connects Us

Illustrations by

## Ellen Rooney

OWLKIDS BOOKS

A park **invites** us—

spreads out its arms and **welcomes** us in,

whoever we are.

A park **greets** us with
"Good day!"
"Buongiorno!"
"Namaste!"
"¿Cómo está?"
"How ya doin', man?"

and gives a grin, a hug, a nod, a wave—
shouts, "You wanna **play?!**"
and always calls out, "**YES!**"

A park **connects** us,
gathers and collects us,
excites us,
**delights** us—

spins and **blows** and **bounces** and **rolls** us.

A park touches us and **teaches** us, inspires and **unleashes** us.

It chirps and blooms and splatters and zooms!

A park can drum out a rhythm
and **dance!**
A park can party.

A park says, "Marry me?" and "I do,"

"Are you hungry?" and "Let's share!"

A park **sings** for peace.
It **marches** for equality.

A park can **also** sit quietly,
holding on to someone's hand,
toes wriggled into sand.

A park **breathes**.
It meanders through the trees.
It purifies and **cleans**.

A park **cradles**
and comforts
and **shelters**
and feeds.

Whoever we are . . .
*However* we are . . .

a park **holds** us
and **heals** us
and **loves** us
and **needs** us.

# Did you know that city parks belong to all of us?

They do! The parks are free to all—and *ours* to share.

But parks did not just magically happen. They were created by people who saw that our cities needed open, green spaces where residents could escape the hustle-bustle and the concrete. These leaders and laborers worked to build and protect our parks so that we could all enjoy them for years to come.

In the middle of the 1800s, North American cities were dirty, crowded, and noisy. They had very few parks for picnicking or playing outdoors. New York City—one of the world's largest cities—was growing by the hour, with new people and businesses. Many New Yorkers were afraid that their city would soon have no green space left at all, just factories, pavement, and buildings, *more* buildings. These New Yorkers wanted a park.

The city bought a long, scraggly rectangle of land in Manhattan, and hired Frederick Law Olmsted to create a park. Olmsted and an architect named Calvert Vaux mapped a plan for what would become Central Park. Over several years, thousands of workers drained swamps, blasted rock, and hauled soil. They built hills, bridges, waterfalls, and walkways, and planted acres and acres of trees, bushes, and wildflowers. At last, the homely rectangle was transformed into a magnificent park, thriving with life.

Soon, other cities wanted magnificent parks of their own. Throughout the next forty years, Olmsted designed hundreds of parks across the U.S. and Canada, from Montreal, Quebec, to Boston, Massachusetts, and Atlanta, Georgia. With each new project, Olmsted shared his grand ideas—that parks should bring us together, connect us to nature, and be shared by *everyone*.

Today, parks continue to connect us. Some cities have created parks in every neighborhood so that *all* people, no matter where we live, have places to relax and play. These smaller neighborhood parks are often filled with green grass and fun things for children, like playgrounds, ball fields, and swimming pools. Toronto, Ontario, has more than 1,500 parks—at least one park for every part of the city.

Many cities around the world have built parks along riverbanks and lakeshores, giving everyone a chance to splash, stroll, and enjoy the waters. Meanwhile, these parks help protect city water from polluted runoff from the streets. Singapore, in Southeast Asia, keeps its water safe to drink by surrounding the city's water reservoirs with vast parkland that also offers hiking trails, a river safari, and a zoo.

Cities everywhere have planted millions of trees with the hope that parks will become the "lungs" of our communities. By filtering soot and smoke and releasing oxygen, trees give city dwellers fresher air to breathe. Chapultepec Forest is one of the world's largest city parks and also acts as a powerful lung for Mexico City. Its canopy of leafy trees helps cool the city and clean the air, while welcoming visitors into a peaceful, green oasis.

Wherever we live, parks make life better. They give us places to play, celebrate, exercise, and unwind. They shelter birds and feed animals. They clean waterways, purify the air, connect us with our neighbors, and unleash us into nature. We *need* our parks. Our parks also need *us*—to use them, appreciate them, share them, and care for them.

While many of us live just a short walk from our nearest city park, there are still places without good parks. Maybe *you* will grow up to be a park maker. What a *magnificent* job that would be.

*For neighbors near and far—may the parks connect us* —S.N.

*For park planners, builders, keepers, and protectors.*
*Thank you for making our parks* —E.R.